Coyote and the Laughing Butterflies

Retold and illustrated by

Harriet Peck Taylor

Macmillan Books for Young Readers
New York

Acknowledgments: I gratefully acknowledge the American Folklore Society for
permission to use this adaptation. I would also like to thank my editor, Anne Dunn,
for her joyous participation every step of the way, and Art Director
Julie Quan, for her inspired sense of design and color.

Macmillan Books for Young Readers
An imprint of Simon & Schuster Children's Publishing Division
Simon & Schuster Macmillan
1230 Avenue of the Americas
New York, New York 10020

Copyright © 1995 by Harriet Peck Taylor

Book design by Julie Y. Quan
The text of this book is set in 16-point Goudy Old Style.
The illustrations were painted on cotton using a batik process:
the patterns and textures were drawn on fabric with hot wax,
then fabric dyes were applied with watercolor brushes.

Printed and bound in Hong Kong by South China
Printing Company (1988) Ltd.
First edition
10 9 8 7 6 5 4 3 2 1

LIBRARY OF CONGRESS CATALOGING-IN-PUBLICATION DATA
Taylor, Harriet Peck.
Coyote and the laughing butterflies / retold and illustrated by
Harriet Peck Taylor.—1st ed.
p.   cm.
Summary: Coyote is tricked by some butterflies who laugh
so hard about their joke that they cannot fly straight.
ISBN 0-02-788846-0
1. Indians of North America—Folklore.   2. Tales—North
America.   [1. Coyote (Legendary character)   2. Indians of North
America—Folklore.   3. Folklore—North America.]   I. Title.
E98.F6T25 1995
398.2'08997—dc20
[E]   94-15278

To my parents,
with love and gratitude for helping me spread my wings

In ancient times, when all the animals could talk, there lived a coyote. Coyote and his wife made their home on top of a grassy mesa surrounded by little hills. A day's journey from their home was a big lake. The water in the lake was so salty that salt crystals collected on the shoreline. Animals came from all around to dig up salt to use for cooking.

One morning Coyote was, as usual, napping in the sun when his wife came to him and said, "Coyote, please go to the big salty lake to get salt for me. I need it for cooking."

Coyote lazily arose, took a sack, and headed for the big salty lake. He followed the trail along the ridge, then around some small hills, through sagebrush, and down into the valley of the big salty lake.

Coyote said to himself, "What a good coyote I am! I've come all this way in the hot sun. I deserve a short rest." He yawned and settled down in the shade of a large cactus. Soon he was fast asleep.

Now in this flower-filled meadow, there lived many beautiful butterflies. One of them flew over Coyote's head and exclaimed, "Look at lazy Coyote, sleeping when he should be gathering salt. Let's play a trick on him!"

The butterflies flew down, and each took hold of a hair in Coyote's fur. In this way, they were able to lift him off the ground.

Coyote snored loudly. *Huh-zzzzz, huh-zzzzz* the butterflies heard as they flew over the mountains and meadows. Finally they dropped him, still asleep, back at his home.

The butterflies flew in crazy patterns in the sky, laughing all the way back to the meadow.

When Coyote woke up, he was very puzzled to find himself back home. He wrinkled his furry forehead and wondered how he had gotten there.

When his wife saw him yawning beside his empty sack, she scolded, "You lazy coyote! Why didn't you get my salt?"

Coyote promised that the very next morning, he would go get the salt.

The next day Coyote awoke bright and early while the sun was still a big orange ball at the edge of the earth. This time he ran faster than tumbleweed as it rolls across the desert. At a bend in the canyon, he saw Lizard lounging lazily on a rock.

"Coyote, my friend, what's your rush? Sit and rest awhile with me on my rock," Lizard said.

"Not today, Lizard. I need to go straight to the big salty lake to get salt!" Coyote shouted as he hurried past.

By the time he got to the lake valley, he was so tired he could barely lift his empty sack. He told himself, "I've got plenty of time. I'll just take a short nap." He was soon sound asleep.

When the butterflies heard Coyote's loud snoring, they decided to play their trick again. One by one they landed on Coyote and lifted him toward white puffy clouds. *Whiissshh* went the wind as it whistled softly through Coyote's fur. He never woke up, not even when he was dropped at home.

The butterflies were laughing hard as they flew away, zigzagging across the sunset sky.

When Coyote's wife came home, she again found him asleep next to his empty sack. Now she was really mad! She sat down next to him with her empty wooden bowl and sighed very loudly.

Coyote awoke and jumped up all at once, rubbing his eyes with his big paws.

"My wife, I am sure that I went to the lake! My legs are stiff and sore from all this running," he told her.

She just shook her head and said, "Coyote, I'll give you one more chance. I need the salt by tomorrow."

"Tomorrow you will have the salt," Coyote promised.

The next day he woke up and stretched his sore muscles. This time he decided not to even follow the trail, but to take a shortcut to the lake. He climbed hills and ran across some little streams, through sagebrush and willows. When he came to the bank of a wide river, his friend Beaver helped him to get across.

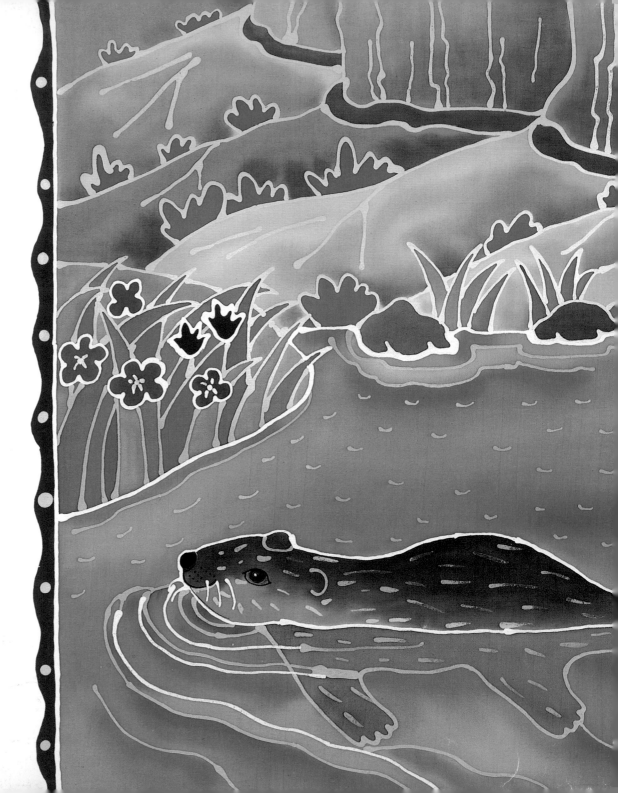

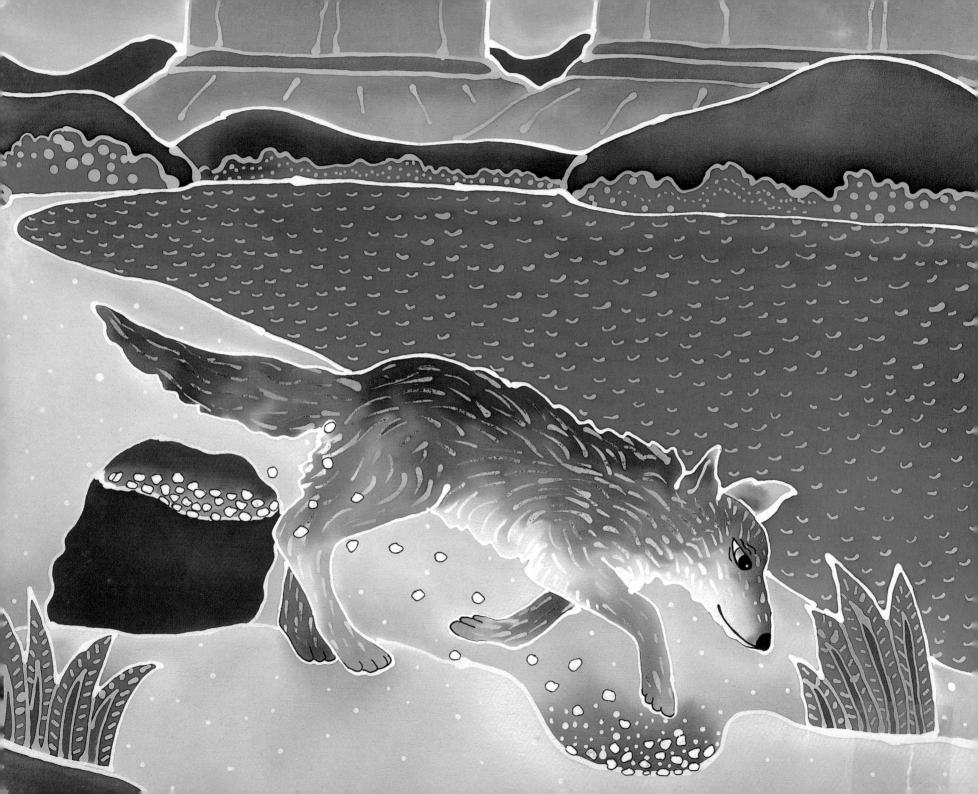

Coyote arrived at the big salty lake more tired than ever. Still determined, he filled his whole sack with salt. My, *what a thoughtful coyote I am! My wife will be so proud of me*, he thought. He decided he had time for just a short nap. His sack made a wonderful pillow, and he was soon sound asleep.

At last the butterflies felt sorry for Coyote. They each grabbed a hair and lifted him once again, but this time some of them also took hold of threads from his heavy salt sack and lifted that, too. Once again they flew over winding canyons and rocky mesas, golden in the evening light.

They dropped him and his sack at home just as the sun was setting.

As soon as he was awake, Coyote saw that he was at home again and yipped in frustration. Then he noticed his sack filled with salt. Now he was really puzzled!

Nevertheless, he took the sack to his wife and said proudly, "I brought you the biggest sack of salt you ever saw!"

She smiled at him and said, "Thank you, Coyote, my husband. I'll start cooking this minute!"

Coyote's wife cooked until she had made enough food to feed herself and Coyote and all their friends. Badger and Bobcat came to the feast, and Roadrunner and Rabbit, and, of course, Lizard, Beaver, and all the beautiful butterflies.

Coyote and his wife shared their food, giving thanks for the harvest. They danced together, nose to nose, coyote-style, as the harvest moon was rising big and orange in that twilight sky.

Even today butterflies remember the trick that was played on Coyote. They flutter high and low, to and fro, laughing too hard to fly straight, all day long in the yellow sunshine.

AUTHOR'S NOTE

The legend on which *Coyote and the Laughing Butterflies* is based comes from the Tewa tribe. The Tewa are a group of Pueblo Indians who live in several villages in northern New Mexico. Around three hundred years ago, some of them migrated and formed an alliance with the Hopi. Over the years these two tribes lived closely and influenced each other, though the Tewa still maintain many of their own customs and ceremonies.

Coyote is a popular character in Pueblo legends as well as in tales of other native peoples. Most often he is called the Trickster. But he is more complicated than that, and therein lies his appeal. He frequently brags and gets himself in trouble, but he is also courageous and has magical powers that he sometimes uses to help others. He does not always follow the rules, but sometimes acts in bold, impulsive ways. Often foolish and lazy, he is full of life and we can see ourselves in him. Coyote makes us laugh and can teach us about ourselves and the world around us.

Other versions of this story can be found in these two sources:

Hayes, Joe. "The Butterflies Trick Coyote," in *A Heart Full of Turquoise: Pueblo Indian Tales*. Sante Fe, N.M.: Mariposa Publishing, 1988.

Parsons, Elise Clews. "Coyote Goes for Salt," in *Tewa Tales*. New York: American Folk-Lore Society, 1926.